# What Did Loonette Forget?
## A Book About Being Thoughtful

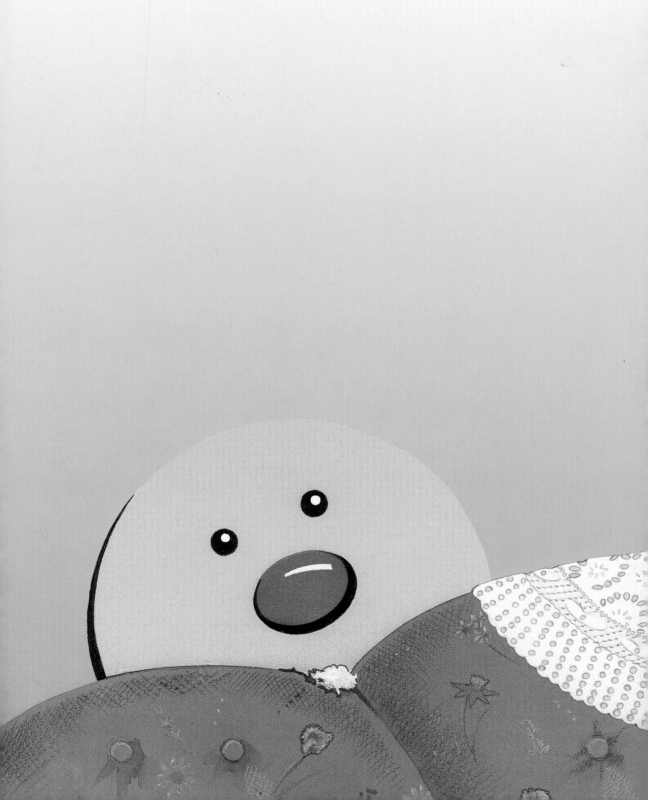

THE BIG COMFY COUCH ™

# What Did Loonette Forget?

## A Book About Being Thoughtful

Written by **Gavin Jackson**

Illustrated by **Richard Kolding**

TIME LIFE Kids

ALEXANDRIA, VIRGINIA

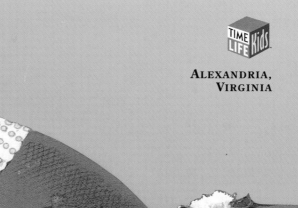

It's morning on the Big Comfy Couch. Loonette the clown and her best friend, Molly, are getting ready for a busy day filled with fun. They stretch and wriggle to shake out all their sleepies. The Dustbunnies under the Couch are waking up too.

After they are all unscrunched, Loonette says, "Molly, it's time for breakfast!"

But what did Loonette forget?

At breakfast, Loonette pours juice, shakes cereal out of the box, and pops toast. "Breakfast gives little clowns energy to work and play all morning long," Loonette tells Molly. "So dig in!"

But what did Loonette forget?

After breakfast, Loonette and Molly go outside to help Granny Garbanzo in her garden. Granny picks a turnip big enough to make a whole tray of turnip tarts.

"Look, Granny," says Loonette. "I picked every red pepper in your garden."

But what did Loonette forget?

Major Bedhead has brought the mail.

"Oooh!" says Loonette. "Look what Auntie Macassar sent! Six silk scarves! They're so beautiful!"

Now Loonette can make a costume for a special dance at Miss Loonette's Dance Academy.

But what did
Loonette forget?

The scarves are just right for Loonette and Molly to do the Dance of the Seven Scarves. "Let's dance, Molly!" cries Loonette.

But what did
Loonette forget?

After Loonette washes her hands and face, she makes some sandwiches.

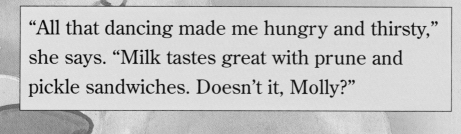

"All that dancing made me hungry and thirsty," she says. "Milk tastes great with prune and pickle sandwiches. Doesn't it, Molly?"

What did Loonette forget?

After lunch is over, Molly and her best clown friend cuddle up on the Big Comfy Couch. They clap to turn on the light.

"Are you ready to hear the story, Molly?" asks Loonette.

But what did
Loonette forget?

After the story, the two best friends are ready to play. But play what?

"I know, Molly," says Loonette. "How about if we let our imagination take us on a trip down a river? The Couch can be our boat!"

To stay safe on their river trip, Molly needs something.

What did Loonette forget?

"Who made this big mess?" Loonette cries. "Oh, right. Me! This room needs a Ten-Second Tidy! I'll put EVERYTHING away!"

But what did
Loonette forget?

After supper, it is time for a bath in the bubble tub. "Baths keep clowns clean and wash away germs," explains Loonette. "That keeps us healthy, Molly. Baths are fun to play in, too!"

But what did
Loonette forget?

After the bath, Loonette helps Molly get dressed for bed. "These are such pretty striped pajamas," she says. "They're all you need to stay nice and warm from head to toe."

But what did Loonette forget?

Loonette hangs up the wet towels and rinses out the bubble tub. "There we are, Molly," she says. "Now we're all finished in the bathroom."

But what did Loonette forget?

At last the busy, happy day is all done. Now Loonette
and Molly must rest up for tomorrow's fun. "Good night,
Molly," says Loonette. "Stay warm!"

What did Loonette forget?

"Sweet dreams, Molly," says Loonette.
"Sleep tight!"

But what did Loonette forget?

"Don't worry, Molly," says Loonette. "I would NEVER forget to kiss you good-night. You're my best doll and I love you. FOREVER and always!"